George Brown, CLASS CLOWN

What's **Black** and White and **Stinks** All Over?

For my parents: Thanks for teaching me that
it's usually better to laugh.–NK

For Little Man Rowan–AB

GROSSET & DUNLAP
Published by the Penguin Group
Penguin Group (USA) Inc., 375 Hudson Street, New York,
New York 10014, USA
Penguin Group (Canada), 90 Eglinton Avenue East, Suite 700,
Toronto, Ontario M4P 2Y3, Canada
(a division of Pearson Penguin Canada Inc.)
Penguin Books Ltd., 80 Strand, London WC2R 0RL, England
Penguin Group Ireland, 25 St. Stephen's Green, Dublin 2, Ireland
(a division of Penguin Books Ltd.)
Penguin Group (Australia), 250 Camberwell Road, Camberwell,
Victoria 3124, Australia
(a division of Pearson Australia Group Pty. Ltd.)
Penguin Books India Pvt. Ltd., 11 Community Centre, Panchsheel Park,
New Delhi—110 017, India
Penguin Group (NZ), 67 Apollo Drive, Rosedale,
North Shore 0632, New Zealand
(a division of Pearson New Zealand Ltd.)
Penguin Books (South Africa) (Pty.) Ltd., 24 Sturdee Avenue,
Rosebank, Johannesburg 2196, South Africa

Penguin Books Ltd., Registered Offices:
80 Strand, London WC2R 0RL, England

Text copyright © 2011 Nancy Krulik. Illustrations copyright © 2011
Aaron Blecha. All rights reserved. Published by Grosset & Dunlap,
a division of Penguin Young Readers Group, 345 Hudson Street,
New York, New York 10014. GROSSET & DUNLAP is a trademark of
Penguin Group (USA) Inc. Printed in the U.S.A.

Library of Congress Control Number: 2010029432

ISBN 978-0-448-45370-5   10 9 8 7 6 5

George Brown, CLASS CLOWN

What's Black and White and Stinks All Over?

by Nancy Krulik

illustrated by Aaron Blecha

Grosset & Dunlap

An Imprint of Penguin Group (USA) Inc.

Chapter 1

Eeerrroooooo!

George Brown covered his ears as feedback from the school intercom exploded into his classroom.

"I think **my ears are bleeding**," George told his friend Alex.

"I'm surprised the noise didn't crack a window," Alex agreed.

"Good morning, students of Edith B. Sugarman Elementary School." The voice of the principal, Mrs. McKeon, was coming through on the intercom. "Here

are your morning announcements: Today's lunch is Salisbury steak."

"Oh man," Alex said. **"Not mystery meat again."**

Salisbury steak was gross. It was always gray and dry. And no matter how much **brown, gooey sauce** was poured over it, it always tasted like cardboard covered in slimy mud.

"First-grade library books should be returned by Friday," the principal continued. "And all third-graders need to remember that their bake sale is next week."

George **started picking dirt** out from under his fingernails. Morning announcements were **so** boring.

"And don't forget, the fourth-grade Field Day is tomorrow," Mrs. McKeon added. "Everyone should arrive at Beaver

Brook Park at nine o'clock sharp. Wear your team shirts and come ready for fun."

George stopped picking at his nails and grinned. This was going to be his first Field Day at his new school. He figured it would be pretty cool.

"What are you smiling about?" Louie, the tall kid who sat near George, whispered. **"Field Day stinks."**

"Come on," George whispered back. "We're going to be outside all day. And we don't get any homework tonight."

"Trust me," Louie said. "It's just a bunch of dumb races and a lousy boxed lunch."

"Yeah, dumb races," Louie's friend Mike said.

"Lousy lunch," Louie's other friend Max added.

George looked over at Alex.

"Louie's right," Alex told George. "And

it usually rains on Field Day, too."

"Please keep it down," their teacher, Mrs. Kelly, said. "Mrs. McKeon hasn't finished all the announcements."

"And now for some big news," Mrs. McKeon continued. "This Friday will be the last time you hear me on the school intercom."

George started to clap and dance around—until he remembered he didn't want to be the class clown anymore. **Those days were over.**

"Starting on Monday, you will find television sets in all of your classrooms," the principal said. "Our school is going to have its own closed-circuit TV station. There will be a studio set up in the audiovisual room. We will be able to broadcast from that studio directly to every classroom in the school!"

George's eyes popped open. A school

TV station. Okay, so maybe this was **a little exciting**.

"The reporters on our new school station will be you—the students," Mrs. McKeon said. "We need writers, camera people, and broadcasters. Anyone interested in being part of WEBS TV should stop by the school office at recess today and sign up."

"Webs TV?" George asked. "What kind of name is that?"

"Not webs," Louie said with a laugh. "W-E-B-S. As in W-Edith B. Sugarman TV. Don't you know anything?"

George did know something. He knew Louie was a **class-A jerk**. But he didn't

say that out loud. Teachers got mad when you said stuff like that. And George was trying really hard not to have any teachers at his new school get mad at him.

George was an expert at being the new kid in school because his dad was in the army, and his family moved around a lot. Up until now, he'd been the class clown at every single school.

This time, though, George was turning over a new leaf. **No more pranks.** No more trips to the principal's office. **No more trouble.**

At first, it really worked. George raised his hand before answering questions. He didn't make faces or laugh behind teachers' backs. He didn't even squirt Jell-O between his teeth and pretend it was blood.

George wasn't causing any trouble. And the **trouble with that** was that the kids all thought he was the boring new guy. But that wasn't the real George **at all**.

Then after his first day at his new school, George's parents took him out to Ernie's Ice Cream Emporium. While they were sitting outside and George was drinking his root beer float, a shooting star flashed across the sky. So George made a wish:

I want to make kids laugh—but not get into trouble.

Unfortunately, the star was gone before George could finish the wish. So only half came true—the first half.

As soon as George had finished his float, **he got a funny feeling in his belly**. It was like hundreds of tiny bubbles were bouncing around in there. The bubbles bounced up and down and all around. They **ping-ponged** their way into his chest and **bing-bonged** their way up into his throat. And then . . .

George let out a big burp. **A *huge* super burp.**

The super burp was loud, and it was *magic*.

Suddenly George lost control of his

arms and legs. It was like they had minds of their own. His hands grabbed straws and stuck them up his nose like a walrus. His feet jumped up on the table and started dancing the **hokey pokey**. Everyone at Ernie's started laughing—  except George's parents, who were covered in the ice cream he had knocked over.

That wasn't the only time the super burp had burst its way out of George's belly. There had been plenty of **magic gas attacks** since then. Once, the burp made him dive-bomb off the stage during the school talent show—which would have been cool if he hadn't landed right in Principal McKeon's lap.

The burp was always popping up when George least expected it. Like the time it came in the middle of his science project and forced him to make his **model volcano** explode all over the classroom. Or the time during the backyard circus when the burp made George jump on a trampoline. He kept bouncing up and down until suddenly, somehow, his underwear got caught on a tree branch. George just hung there with the **world's worst wedgie**. His rear end still hurt whenever he thought about it!

To make matters worse, Louie always made fun of George for the things the burp made him do. Goofing on George was Louie's favorite hobby. George didn't know why Louie hated him so much. **But Louie did hate him.** He'd even thrown George out of his band—for no reason at all, except that he hated George.

Which was actually kind of okay, because George wasn't too crazy about Louie, either. In fact, Louie was the **worst thing** about living in Beaver Brook. Well, except for the magic super burp.

Chapter 2

"What are you guys signing up for?"
George asked Alex and Chris as they
headed toward the school office after
lunch.

"Cameraman," Alex said.

"I want to be a news reporter," Chris
said.

George looked down and scraped some
Salisbury steak goo from his shirt. Then
he popped his finger in his mouth. *Yuck.*

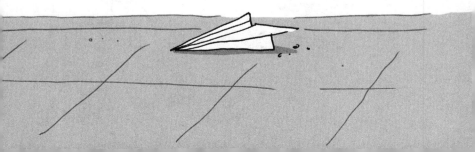

It still tasted like brown, gooey slime. But what tasted even worse than the goo? **The goo mixed with shirt lint.**

George gagged a little and swallowed. Then he said, "I think I'd make a good sportscaster."

"Why?" Chris asked.

"I love skateboarding," George said. "That counts as a sport."

"Yeah, but you'd have to report on the school basketball team and the track team," Alex told him. "We don't have a skateboard team."

"I was on the track team at my old school," George said. He didn't add that he usually came in last in every race. **That was the one good thing about being the new kid.** No one in your new school had to know any of the embarrassing junk that happened at your old school.

In the school office, a **really tall** sixth-grader came over to George and his friends. "Are you guys here to sign up for the TV station?" he asked.

Alex said, "I was thinking about being a cameraman."

"We still have a couple of spots open," the kid said. "And since you're a fourth-grader, you can work the cameras. No one in the lower grades is allowed to."

"Cool," Alex said. "What do I do?"

The kid pointed to sign-up sheets that were taped to the wall. "Write your name on the one that says CAMERAS."

"Do you still need news reporters?" Chris asked.

"Do you have any experience?" the big sixth-grader asked.

Chris didn't say anything. George could tell he was kind of scared. The sixth-grader was huge.

"Chris is a *great* writer," George piped up. "He writes comic books. They're about this **superhero** named **Toiletman**, who uses a plunger to flush out trouble."

The sixth-grader frowned. "Writing news stories is different from writing comic stories about a guy with a plunger."

"A *superhero* with a plunger," George corrected him.

"Whatever." The kid looked at Chris. "I guess we could give you a try," he said finally.

As Chris wrote his name on the sign-up sheet, George swallowed hard and said, "I'd really like to be a sportscaster."

"You and about a billion other kids," the sixth-grader said. "There's only going

to be one sportscaster from each grade."

"Has anybody else from the fourth grade signed up?" George asked. Then, out of the corner of his eye, George spotted Louie coming into the school office. He was with Mike and Max, just like always.

"Okay, I already signed my name on the sheet," Louie told the sixth-grader. "So when can I do my first sportscast?"

Oh man. Louie had beaten him to the sign-up sheet.

"Not so fast," the sixth-grader said. "This kid here wants the job; other kids do, too."

Louie glared at George. **"He doesn't have the experience I have,"** he told the sixth-grader.

"What experience?" George asked him.

"My brother, Sam, is the sportscaster at the middle school TV station," Louie explained.

"It's a family thing," Mike said.

"Kind of like big noses," Max said. "Not that you have a big nose or anything, Louie," he added quickly.

"We've gotta make this fair," the sixth-grader said.

"Well, I got here first," Louie said. "So I'm the sportscaster, **fair and square.**"

"You eat faster than me is all," George said. "So you got here quicker."

Just then Principal McKeon walked out of her office. "What's the problem, boys?"

"They both want to be the fourth-grade sportscaster," the big kid explained.

Mrs. McKeon nodded. "Well, how about making an **audition tape**?"

"How would we do that?" George asked her.

"Tomorrow is Field Day," Mrs. McKeon said. "Anyone who wants to be the fourth-grade sportscaster should report on the events."

"How are we supposed to report on the races when we're running in them?" George asked.

Mrs. McKeon said, "You can report on the races you aren't taking part in. You can interview your friends, too."

"That sounds fair," George said.

The sixth-grader shrugged. "Okay. After I watch the tapes, I'll decide who made **the best one**, and that kid gets the job."

George held his hand out to Louie. "May the best man win."

"Oh, I will," Louie said.

"Yeah, he will," Max added.

"Definitely," Mike agreed. "Louie always wins."

George smiled. *Not this time,* he thought.

Chapter 3

When George arrived at Beaver Brook Park the next morning, he saw Louie showing Mike how to use a fancy video camera. It was the kind of video camera that could shoot things from far away and close-up. It seemed like Mike was having a really tough time learning how to use it.

It wasn't right that **such a jerk** had so much cool stuff. Louie had been the first kid in the grade to get **sneakers with wheels on them**. He was the first one to get a scooter with a motor on it. And now he was the first kid to have a superdeluxe video camera.

"You better take real good care of that camera," Louie told Mike. "It's my brother, Sam's."

"I will," Mike promised. "I swear."

"And make sure you point the camera at me **a lot**, and use that close-up lens," Louie told him. "This is *my* audition tape."

"Close-ups, got it," Mike said.

"What can I do, Louie?" Max asked.

Louie thought for a minute. "You make sure my hair looks good and stuff like that while Mike is shooting me."

Max nodded. "You can count on me!"

he said. "You can have my napkin at lunch, too, so you don't get any stains on your shirt."

"All my folks had was this old camera," Alex said to George. "My mom got it when I was born."

"It's okay," George said. "You're definitely going to be a better cameraman than Mike. Besides, it's not how good the camera is. It's how good the *sportscaster* is. Who are people going to want to get their sports news from—a cool kid like me or a **pain in the neck** like Louie?"

Just then Sage snuck up behind George and Alex. "**Georgie**, I heard you're trying to be a sportscaster," she said. "I'm in the wheelbarrow race. Do you want to interview me now?"

George turned around. Sage was tilting her head and giving him a goofy smile.

"Well, uh . . . **no thanks**," George mumbled. "Maybe later."

"I'm so glad we're on the same team," Sage continued, pointing to her T-shirt. It was green with white letters that said Vipers, just like George's shirt. "I don't like snakes. But I'll wear the shirt proudly **because *you're* wearing it, too**."

At first, George thought he was lucky to be on the Vipers, especially since Alex

and Chris had wound up on that team, too. But now that George knew Sage was on his team, **he wasn't so cool with it anymore**.

Then again, at least he wasn't on the other team, **the Sharks**, with Louie, Max, and Mike. George's friend Julianna was on their team, though.

Too bad the Vipers couldn't trade Sage for Julianna. She was a lot cooler

than Sage was. She was also **a lot faster** than just about anyone in the fourth grade. A kid like Julianna could win Field Day for her team.

"Boys and girls, gather around!" Principal McKeon shouted through her megaphone. "It's time to start the Field Day festivities."

"What's Principal McKeon doing here?" George asked Chris and Alex.

"Since your gym teacher, Mr. Trainer, is absent today—," Mrs. McKeon continued.

George started to laugh. The whole time George had been at Edith B. Sugarman Elementary School, he'd only seen Mr. Trainer a couple of times. The guy was always absent.

"I am going to lead you kids in a **special sun salutation**," Mrs. McKeon said.

Sage started hopping up and down like she had just heard the best news in the world. "Oh yay!" she cheered. "I love yoga. **You get to twist your body into all sorts of shapes.** The sun salutation is tough, though."

Just then, Louie came running over. Mike and Max were right behind him.

"So, you know how to do this yoga pose, Sage?" Louie asked.

Louie was making his voice sound really low. George figured he was trying to sound like a real sportscaster.

"I take classes," Sage told him. "And I'm really good. Yoga helps you to be at one with nature, **which is perfect**, since we're out here with all this nature around."

George wanted to stick his finger down his throat and pretend he was puking, but he didn't. If the principal saw him, she'd be mad. **And he was trying really hard not to get in trouble.**

Sage showed the kids a couple of yoga poses. "This is cobra," she said as she got down on her belly and lifted her head like a snake.

"Film her!" Louie snapped at Mike.

Rats. George had to admit Louie had beaten him to **the first scoop of the day**.

Not that he was sure yoga counted as a sport. *But still.*

"Okay, kids," Mrs. Kelly said as she walked over to where Sage was demonstrating her **downward-facing dog**. "Let's all gather around Mrs. McKeon so we can do our sun salutations."

George looked at Mrs. Kelly's T-shirt. It had green and white stripes on it. Mrs. McKeon was wearing the same shirt, and so was Mrs. Miller, the other fourth-grade teacher. George figured that showed that the teachers and the principal **weren't taking sides**.

"Okay, fourth-graders, first we stand up straight with our hands together," Mrs. McKeon explained as she started the sun salutation. "Next we reach up high toward the sun . . ."

George tried to follow the yoga poses his principal was doing.

The hardest one was downward-facing dog.

George tried to bend over and stick his rear end in the air like a dog stretching after a nap. But he couldn't. He was too freaked out by **the bubbles starting to fizz in his belly**.

George could tell there was a burp brewing down there. And not just any burp. From the way those bubbles were bing-bonging their way around his belly, George could tell this was a *super burp*. And that was *ba-a-ad*!

George was going to have to fight with all his might to keep it down. Because if **George couldn't squelch this belch**, there was going to be trouble!

The last thing George wanted was for the super burp to escape in front of the whole fourth grade. He clamped his lips tight and sucked in his belly as hard as he could. And then . . .

George let out the loudest burp anyone had ever heard. It was so loud **you could hear it on the sun**!

The kids all turned around to stare at him. George opened his mouth and tried to say "excuse me." But all that came out was, *"Ruff! Ruff!"*

It wasn't George's fault. It was his *mouth's* fault. But it didn't want to apologize. It wanted to bark like a

downward-facing dog.

"Ruff! Ruff!"

George ordered himself to stand up and act **normally**. But that didn't happen. Instead, George stayed down on all fours. He ran over to a tree. Then he lifted his leg and pretended to be **a dog peeing on the tree**.

The kids' mouths all hung open. *Was this really happening?*

"George Brown!" Principal McKeon shouted. "That's not funny!"

"Arooo!" George howled.

He rolled over in the grass.

He sat up on his hind legs. He pushed his tongue out of his mouth, held his arms out like a dog, and begged.

The kids all laughed harder.

"Stop that right now!" Principal McKeon shouted.

"Yip! Yip!" George barked.

His arms and legs raced over to Principal McKeon. **And then George's tongue did the worst thing EVER.**

It licked Principal McKeon's hand! **Gross!** Now George had principal germs in his mouth. But George's tongue didn't care. It just kept licking.

And then . . . suddenly . . . *Whoosh!* George felt a huge bubble **pop** inside his stomach. All the air rushed right out of him.

The super burp was gone

But George was still ther

a little whimper—kind of lik

saying he was sorry. But it w

apologize.

From the look on Principal McKeon's
face, George could tell **he was in trouble**.
Big trouble. He wasn't sure what
punishment the principal was going to dish
out. But he was pretty sure it would be *ruff*.

Chapter 4

George was sitting on a rock with his head in his hands. "She's **calling my parents** tonight," George told Alex. "They'll probably **ground me for a week**." George groaned. "And she penalized our team two points."

"That was severe," Alex said. "All you did was bark a little."

George knew that wasn't all he'd done. Alex was just trying to make him feel better.

But **the worst part** was that Louie was interviewing kids about George. "So, what just happened out there?" Louie asked Julianna.

"I think George was trying to psych out our team," Julianna said. "He wanted us to think he was a **wild, crazy dog** who was

dangerous. But we're the Sharks. We're not afraid of anyone."

Louie smiled. Then he turned to Chris and Alex. **"Hey, did you know our team has a secret weapon?** It's George. As long as he's on your side, *we're* sure to win."

That really cracked up Mike and Max. Mike laughed so hard, he almost dropped the video camera.

Louie shot him an angry look. Mike stopped laughing. Fast.

George pretended to ignore Louie. He turned to watch some other kids get ready at the starting line for the **wheelbarrow race**. Chris was the wheelbarrow, and Sage was holding his legs.

Mrs. McKeon blew her whistle and the kids took off down the field. It was an exciting race. It could actually make a good story for his sportscast audition tape.

"Alex, turn on the camera and follow me," he said.

Alex grabbed the camera and began filming George as he ran along the side of the field.

"There's Sage pushing Chris as hard as she can," George said, **sounding like a real sportscaster**. "Notice how straight Chris is holding his legs. That's how the professional wheelbarrow racers do it."

George asked Alex to switch his camera angle. "Oh, look! Louie and

Julianna are coming up from the rear.
Julianna is the wheelbarrow and she's
working hard at walking on her hands.
But Louie has just dropped her legs.
Oooh. Belly flop! **That had to hurt.**"

George and Alex ran ahead to watch
the winners crossing the finish line.
"Watch out, Sage and Chris," he said into
the camera. "Louie and Julianna are right
beside you. **It's anyone's race now!**"

A split second later, Sage, Chris, Louie, and Julianna all made it to the finish line.

"We won!" Sage and Chris shouted excitedly.

"We won!" Louie and Julianna shouted excitedly.

"I think it was a tie," Mrs. McKeon told the kids.

George said, "Look, **Alex shot the whole thing**. We were filming the race. That will show who won."

"Terrific, George," Mrs. Kelly told him. "Principal McKeon and I will watch the tape now."

Alex handed over his camera, and a few moments later, Mrs. McKeon said, **"Well, this decides it.** Sage's hand crossed the finish line just a second before Julianna's. Chris and Sage are the winners. Good reporting, George."

As soon as Mrs. Kelly and Principal McKeon had walked away, Louie gave George an angry look.

"I bet you **got yourself kicked out** of the race on purpose."

"Why would I do that?" George asked.

"Because you want to be the sportscaster," Louie said. **"That was probably the most exciting race of the day.** I was racing so I couldn't report on it."

George grinned. That was true. And there was nothing Louie could do about it.

Chapter 5

"Go-o-o-o-o Vipers!" George and Chris
gave each other a high five as **George
crossed the finish line**—just seconds
ahead of Louie—in the final leg of the relay
race. Now George had made up those two
points he'd lost for the Vipers earlier.

And the best part was that Alex had picked up the camera **just in time** to film George winning for his team. George would be able to use his own victory in his audition tape. **Sweet!**

Soon it was time for the next race. A large, brown suitcase was placed on the ground in front of each team. "What's that for?" George asked his teammates.

"A race," Sage told him.

George rolled his eyes. *No duh.* "What *kind* of race?"

"I don't have a clue," Alex said.

Just then, Mrs. McKeon picked up a megaphone. She looked at the Vipers. Then she looked at the Sharks. "Okay, fourth-graders," she said. "For this race, one person on each team has to be *it*. Are there any volunteers?"

George smiled. Here was his chance to really get everyone on his good side.

He would volunteer to be *it*—even though **he had no real idea** what he was volunteering for.

"Me. I'll do it," he told the other Vipers.

"I'll be *it* for the Sharks," Julianna volunteered. She smiled over at George. "It's you against me."

"The object of this race is to dress the person who is *it*," Mrs. McKeon continued. "You must put **every piece of clothing in the suitcase** on him or her. And then, once that person is dressed, he or she has to run to the finish line."

George smiled. That didn't sound too hard.

But the minute Mrs. Kelly blew her whistle and Alex opened the suitcase, **George knew he was in trouble**. There weren't just any clothes inside the suitcase. There were *lady's* clothes:

a dress, a pocketbook, a shawl, a curly
blond wig, and **worst of all** . . . high
heels. Was George actually supposed to
run in them?

The minute the whistle blew, Chris
picked up a yellow and red flowered dress
and shoved it over George's head. **"Suck
in your gut, George,"** Chris told him. **"I
gotta zip this thing."**

"Okay, here's your shawl," Sage
said. "Oh, I love how you look in purple,
George."

Alex dumped the wig on George's
head. "Wow! You're a blonde!"

"Ha-ha. Very funny," George said as he slipped on the high-heeled shoes.

"Now grab your pocketbook and run!" Chris said. He started to laugh. "Man, that sounds hilarious."

George could barely walk. And he couldn't see. He took two steps. *Whoops!* He fell backward **right onto his rear end**. But he scrambled up, straightened his wig, held tight to his purse, and kept on hobbling toward the finish line.

Once or twice he looked back. Thank goodness Julianna wasn't having any better luck than George. She was falling all over the place, too.

"Come on, George, just a few more feet!" Alex shouted.

George **huffed** and **puffed**. He pushed the wig out of his eyes. He put **one heel in front of the other**.

Ooomph. George fell right on his belly.

He reached his arms out to break his fall. And then . . .

"We have a winner!" Mrs. McKeon shouted. "George's hand has just crossed the finish line. The Vipers win!"

George looked up. Through the

strands of yellow wig-hair he could see his teammates **cheering wildly**.

He could also see Louie. He was yelling at Mike and pointing at George. "Not me!" Louie shouted. "Point the camera at George!"

As Mike videotaped George, Louie began talking in his sportscaster voice. "It was close. Julianna would have won, if George—or should I call him *Georgina*—hadn't **belly flopped** over the finish line."

As Mike turned off the camera, Louie

shoved his face right into George's and shot
him a mean grin. "This is going to be the
best **sports blooper tape** anyone has ever
made! I can't wait until the whole school
sees it."

Blooper tape! So that was what Louie was
up to. He was using this sportscaster contest
as another excuse to make fun of George.

Grrr . . .

Chapter 6

"There goes Chris!" George announced as Alex filmed the **egg-on-a-spoon** race. "He's gaining on Mike. Oops. Chris lost his egg. And this race goes to the Sharks."

Chris was not smiling after he crossed the finish line a couple of feet behind Mike. "That's harder than it looks," he told George and Alex.

"Don't worry, dude," George told him. "The next race is the three-legged race. I did that with my dad at an army base picnic. **I can win it for us.**"

Just then, Sage walked over to George. She had a thick rope in her hands. "I'll be your partner, George," she said. Then she **batted her eyelashes** up and down. It made her look like she had spider legs hanging from her eyelids. *Yuck!*

Mrs. Kelly flashed one of her **big, gummy smiles** at George and Sage. "How nice!" she said. "I didn't know you two were such good friends."

George was really stuck now. He was going to have to touch Sage—*ugh!*—whether he liked it or not.

A few minutes later, George and Sage hobbled **arm in arm** over to the starting line, right next to Louie and Max. Louie looked over and flashed George a big smile. George didn't know why.

"Okay, everyone," Principal McKeon said. **"On your mark . . . get set . . . go!"**

George and Sage took off down the field. They were going pretty fast, too. At least they were until George felt something fizzy in his belly.

Oh no! Not the **super burp**!

But it *was* the super burp. It was back, and **it wanted out**. Already it was

ping-ponging its way out of George's belly, and **bing-bonging** its way into his chest.

This could get really *ba-a-ad*!

George had to keep the burp down. It had already gotten him in trouble once today. **Once was enough.**

George shut his mouth tight. He started banging on his chest. Maybe he could **break up the burp** and push it back down into his belly.

Oomph! George hit himself again and lost his balance.

To keep from falling, George grabbed on
to **whatever was closest**—which happened
to be Sage.

Sage wrapped her arms around George
and gave him a squeeze. **"Oh, Georgie!"**

Everyone was looking!

This was terrible. Horrible. Awful.

Whoosh! Suddenly George felt a huge bubble pop inside his stomach. All the air rushed right out of him. **The fizzy feeling was gone.**

Louie and Mike won the race. But at least George had squelched the belch!

Sage was smiling. She batted her eyelashes up and down. "I knew you liked me," she told him, and gave him a hug.

George groaned. The belch was gone, but Sage was **making him sick** to his stomach.

"Did you get all of it on camera?" Louie was asking Mike. "Me winning *and* that clown freaking out again?" Louie was pointing at George.

"Every second," Mike said proudly. "Even the hug."

"I wasn't hugging her!" George insisted as he untied himself from Sage.

"You were, too!" Sage said. **Then she stormed off.**

George tried to look on the bright side. The **really important thing** was that he'd managed to beat the burp. And as an added bonus, maybe now Sage would leave him alone.

Score one for George!

Chapter 7

"Dude, what came over you? You were **definitely acting weird** out there," Alex told George as the boys took their boxed lunches to a far corner of the field.

"You'd act weird, too, if you were tied to Sage," George said as he plopped on the ground. He opened the cardboard box and looked inside. *Yuck!*

He picked up the squished pieces of bread. "What's inside this?"

Chris took a look at his sandwich. "At first I thought it was egg salad because **there's something yellow in it**," he said. "But now I'm not so sure."

"What are those gray spots on the bread?" Alex asked.

"Better not to know," George answered.

"I think that piece of celery just moved," Chris said.

George looked down at Chris's sandwich. **"Dude, I don't think that's celery,"** he said, and put his sandwich back in the box. "Can I borrow the camera?" he asked Alex.

"Are you going to film people eating?" Chris asked him.

"Eating's not a sport," Alex told Chris.

"It is when you eat this stuff," George joked. "You take a bite and then see how fast you can run to the bathroom to **throw up**."

Alex and Chris laughed.

"Actually, I'm going to interview people about how they think the day is going," George told his friends. "Because so far I only have the wheelbarrow race. And Louie has . . ." George couldn't even finish the sentence. It was that **embarrassing**.

Instead, he pointed the camera at Chris. "So, Chris, can you tell me what the **highlight of the morning** was for you?"

"Well, I kind of liked zipping you into that dress for the race," Chris said with a laugh. "That was hilarious."

George turned the camera away from Chris. Fast. "How about you, Alex?" he asked, pointing the camera at his other best friend.

"It was pretty funny the way you did the downward-facing dog," Alex said. "Licking Principal McKeon's hand—**that took guts**."

This interview was *not* going the way George had hoped.

"Check it out," Chris said. "Louie saw you interviewing us, so now he's interviewing people on his team. **That guy doesn't have an original idea in his head**."

"It doesn't matter," Alex told him. Then

he smiled. "Guess what? Mike forgot to turn the camera on. The little red light isn't flashing now. The **tape's gonna be blank**."

"Louie's going to freak when he realizes Mike's not getting any of this," Chris said.

"I hope so," George said. "Because *that's* something I'd really like to get on tape!"

Chapter 8

"Wow! **This is a race worthy of Toiletman!**" Chris shouted excitedly as he and the other Vipers gathered at the starting line for the first race after lunch.

On the ground in front of each team was **a plunger and three rolls of toilet paper**.

Mrs. McKeon picked up her megaphone.

"This race is always a favorite at Field Day," Mrs. McKeon announced, a big smile on her face. "There will be three contestants from each team. **The first person scoops up a roll of toilet paper onto the plunger end.** Then he or she runs across the field, dumps the toilet paper in the trash bucket, and races back to the starting line so the second person can do the same thing. The first team to get all three rolls into their trash bucket wins!"

"Oh, we're gonna win this one," Chris said. **"Toilet paper is my thing!"**

"Then you should go first," Alex told Chris. "And then maybe Sage can go." Alex turned to a skinny kid with really long legs. "Charlie, you go last. You'll be running against Julianna, which will be hard."

"I think I can beat her," Charlie said.

George smiled. The Vipers just might be able to take this race.

The whistle blew and the race began!

"Chris is off to a great start," George said. "Look at his technique. The roll of toilet paper is sitting right in the middle of the plunger. **He's got it perfectly balanced! What skill!**"

At first, George was smiling for the camera. But then, all of a sudden, he didn't feel like smiling anymore. That fizzy feeling was back. It wasn't just

bing-bonging and ping-ponging its way
up to George's mouth. This time it was
BING-BONGING and PING-PONGING!

**This was a classic battle between
man and burp!** And it was a fight George
was determined to win. Quickly, he
grabbed a roll of toilet paper and shoved a
wad in his mouth like a cork.

"George, **quit kidding around**,"
Charlie said. "That toilet paper is for the
race."

But George *wasn't* kidding around.
This was serious business. He stuffed

more and more toilet paper into his mouth. **His cheeks felt like they were about to explode.**

Alex couldn't help himself. He began to laugh really hard.

"Alex, stop laughing!" Sage said. "Chris is almost back with the plunger. I'm next."

George could feel his eyes bulging now. The **burp was really angry**. It was pounding around in George's chest and bouncing up into his throat. *Boing! Boing! Boing!*

The **magic burp** slipped out. It wasn't a huge burp. In fact, as far as super burps went, it was kind of small. But it was powerful enough to shoot the wad of wet, slimy toilet paper **out of George's mouth** and into the air.

Splat! The wad of paper and spit landed **right on the back of Louie's neck**.

"Hey! Who did that?" Louie turned around and glared.

George opened his mouth to say "sorry." But that's not what came out. Instead, George's mouth started to tell jokes.

"Speaking of toilet paper," George's mouth said, "do you guys know why Eeyore looked into the toilet? He wanted to see Pooh!"

Some kids on the Vipers laughed. But most were cheering Sage on. She was running down the field with the **toilet paper sitting on her plunger**. As soon as she reached the starting line, she handed

the plunger off to Charlie. Charlie scooped up the toilet paper on the plunger.

"You guys know what one toilet said to the other?" George asked his teammates. **"You sure you're not sick?** You're looking a little flushed!"

Charlie was running down the field, but he was laughing so hard he dropped the toilet paper . . . twice.

"George, I know you're having fun," Mrs. Kelly said. "But **this is still school**. That kind of joke just isn't appropriate."

"Then **how about this one**?" George's mouth asked. "What game is played in the bathroom?"

"What?" Alex asked.

"Ring Around the Bathtub," George said.

The kids laughed again. Mrs. Kelly said, "I think it's time to stop joking now."

Suddenly, the Sharks began to cheer. Julianna had crossed the finish line. She'd won the race for her team.

Whoosh! Something went pop in the bottom of George's belly. It was like all the air rushed right out of him. The burp was gone.

George opened his mouth to say "sorry." **And that's exactly what came out.** He was sorry that the Vipers had lost the race.

"I hope you're apologizing for spitting toilet paper at me," Louie shouted to George.

George shook his head. "Don't blame me," he said. After all, George hadn't spit anything at anyone. The super burp had **blasted the paper** right out of him.

Louie glared at George. "You're just lucky Mike was running in the race so he couldn't film you. Otherwise, I would prove it was you who spit toilet paper at me."

"I'm not sure who did what," Mrs. Kelly told the boys. "But I'm keeping my eye on you, George Brown. Trouble seems to follow you wherever you go."

George frowned. It wasn't trouble that was following him. **It was gas.**

Chapter 9

"Does everyone have their paint chips?" Alex asked. "The scavenger hunt is worth three points. If we take this, we're the **Field Day champions**."

"All right!" George pumped his fist in the air. His team still had a chance.

George held his white and yellow chips. Each kid had two paint chips in different colors. The idea was to find **something in nature** that matched the colors you were holding.

"Okay, fourth-graders, start hunting!" Mrs. McKeon shouted cheerfully.

Sage showed her orange and purple chips to George. "Purple is going to be hard." She smiled, and started doing that **spider-leg-eyelash-blinking thing again**. "Maybe you can help me."

Yeah, like that was going to happen. George wasn't planning on staying anywhere near Sage. He started running and didn't look back.

When he figured he was far enough away, George stopped and took out his paint chips. Yellow. That shouldn't be too hard. He looked around in the grass until he spotted **a bright yellow dandelion**. It was the exact shade of yellow that he needed. **Oh yeah!** *Score!*

"Yellow dandelion!" George said as he went over to Chris and dropped the weed into the Vipers' brown paper bag his friend was holding.

"And here's a green leaf," Charlie said. He held it next to his paint chip. **"It's an exact match."**

"I've got brown . . . here's some brown . . . *something*," Chris said.

He stared at
what looked like a pile of
dark brown pebbles.
Alex glanced over Chris's shoulder.
"That's poop," he said. He bent down
and took a closer look. **"It probably
comes from a medium-sized
rodent."**

George looked at his
friend in amazement. Alex
was smart. But this was
creepy **smart.** "You can
actually tell what made
this poop?"

"Not exactly," Chris said.
"But judging from the poop's
color and its smell, it's definitely
a rodent. Probably one that eats

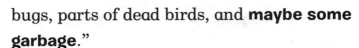

bugs, parts of dead birds, and **maybe some garbage**."

"Okay, I think I'm going to throw up," said Sage, who had suddenly appeared.

"Just scoop the poop and stick it in the bag, Chris," George said. "We have to move fast if we're going to win the scavenger hunt."

"I'm not scooping up any poop," Chris said. "You do it."

"No way," George said.

"Don't look at me," Sage told the boys.

"Alex?" George asked. **"You're the poop expert around here."**

"I only look," Alex said. "I don't touch."

"Maybe I'd better find something else **dark brown**," Chris said.

"Look! **There's fungus** on the roots of that

tree," George told him. "It's dark brown."

Chris started pointing to the bushes nearby. "Hey, did you guys hear that?" he asked.

"Hear what?" George asked.

The kids all got very quiet. Suddenly **there was some rustling in the bushes**. There was definitely something hiding.

"Maybe it's whatever made that poop," George said.

"Let's go." Sage tugged at George's

sleeve. George pulled away from her.

"You think it's **a bear** or something?" Chris asked nervously. "I saw this movie once where a bear tore apart a whole family." Chris started walking in the opposite direction. **"I'm outta here."**

"Good idea," Alex said.

"I'm right behind you," George agreed.

"And I'm right behind *you*, George," Sage said.

George groaned.

Chapter 10

"Mud! Nice, brown mud," Chris shouted. He reached down and scooped up a handful of **slippery, slimy lake mud**, and plopped it into the scavenger hunt bag. "One color closer to victory!"

George hunted all around the edge of the lake for something that was white. Sage found a purple flower, so she was done. Alex found a gray rock and a blue feather. And Charlie had already picked a red berry from a bush. But nothing white was in sight . . . **it was weird**. Back home in his dresser there were a million things that were white, or sort of white: his socks, his T-shirts, even his **tighty-whitey underpants**. Out here, nothing.

George sat down on a hollow log to think. But before he could investigate further, he heard a loud, rumbling sound. And that was scary because of where it was coming from.

The rumbling was coming from George's belly—along with a terrible, fizzy feeling. The kind of feeling George always got when he **let loose a mighty, mega, magical super burp**.

Oh no! He was setting **some sort of record** for magic burps in a single day! Already it was ping-ponging its way out of George's belly and bing-bonging its way into his chest.

George wasn't about to surrender to the burp. He **clamped his mouth shut** and **sucked in his stomach** as hard as he could. He spun around and around in a circle, trying to force the burp into his feet like water down a drain.

The spinning was a bad move. Now,
besides feeling fizzy, George felt dizzy.

Sage went running over. "George, are
you okay?" she asked.

George stared right at Sage and . . .

B·U·U·U·R·P!

He let out a **massive** burp.

"Gross!" Sage shouted.

George opened his mouth to
say "excuse me." But that's
not what came out. Instead,

George shouted, "CANNONBALL!"

George's legs sprang into action. They raced to the lake. And then, **with one powerful leap**, his legs catapulted him into it.

"Yo, dude, get out of there," Alex called. "We've got a job to do!"

George wanted to get out of the water. He really did. **But George wasn't in charge of George now.** The super burp was. And it had other plans.

George's body ducked down under the water. A moment later, he popped back up and began **spitting a stream of water** right out of his mouth. He was a giant George fountain. Now kids from the other team came to watch the *George Show*.

As soon as **the George fountain was empty**, George's legs ran out of the lake and onto the shore. Chris was shouting and pointing at something . . .

George shook the water out of his ears. Now he could hear. Chris was shouting, **"Skunk!"**

Kids scattered as fast as their legs would take them. All except for George.

Skunks were black . . . and white! Maybe he could get **some white skunk hair** and win the scavenger hunt for his team.

Part of George's brain knew this was crazy thinking. But the burp had taken over his mind now, too! He scurried over to the skunk.

The skunk glared at George. George glared back. All he needed was one skunk hair. He reached out . . . and the skunk turned around and **pointed its black-and-white-striped tush** right at George. Then it raised its tail and **let out a spray.**

Whoosh! George felt something go pop in his belly—**like a pin going into a balloon**. All the air seemed to just rush right out of him.

The super burp was gone . . . but the smell of the **skunk spray** was not!

George stank, stunk, or however you say it . . . "Oh man," he groaned. **He was wet, smelly, and miserable.**

Just when George thought nothing could be worse, he heard a noise coming from nearby.

And then something awful emerged from behind the bushes. Something worse than a bear. **Worse than a wild coyote. Even worse than a skunk.**

It was a *Louie*!

"George, that was awesome!" Louie shouted. "Mike, did you get that?" he asked.

Mike popped out of the bushes. "Yep, I got the whole thing on film."

Max popped out of the bushes, too.

"So, it was you hiding in there?" George asked.

"Yeah," Louie said. "I had to sneak around. How else"—he paused to scratch at his face—"was I going to get **secret footage** of you being a jerk again?"

Mike scratched his arm and held up the camera. "I'd show it to you, but I don't want to get too close. **You stink.**" He turned to Louie and smiled. "The camera was set on *record* this time—I checked."

"Awesome," Louie told him.

Oh man. George was never going to be able to live *this* down.

"FIELD DAY STINKS!" he shouted.

Chapter 11

Mrs. Kelly and Mrs. McKeon decided it
was best for George to leave Field Day early.
So while the rest of his team were declared
the Field Day winners (Alex had managed to
find a white pebble by the shore of the lake),
George was on his way home. He stunk **so
badly** that his own *mom* made him ride his
bike while she followed in the car.

Everywhere George rode, people dived out of the way. Babies in strollers held their noses. Squirrels raced up into trees **when they smelled him coming**!

Not that George blamed them. He would have moved out of his own way, too, if he could have.

At home, George had to take a bath in tomato juice. The juice was thick and pulpy. It got stuck in his hair and between his toes. And the juice didn't even really get rid of the skunk stink. George just wound up smelling like **a tomato-covered skunk**.

Yo, Kevin,

I got sprayed by a skunk today. It smelled so nasty! And the only thing that would get rid of the skunky smell was tomato juice. I had to take a bath in it. My mom poured gallons of tomato juice into the tub, and then I got in . . . I hated it. But I know you would have loved it because you are so crazy about tomatoes.

Your pal,
George

George knew only one person in the whole world who would have had fun getting rid of the smell of skunk: his friend at his old school, Kevin Camilleri. So George wrote and told him all about it.

George didn't go to school the **next day**. He had to stay home until he smelled **less skunky**. Ordinarily that would have made George happy. Just not *that* day. It was the day he was supposed to hand in his sports tape. But since he was absent, **he was out of luck**. Now Louie was going to get to be the fourth-grade sportscaster, after all. That stunk, too. Alex called George right after school. **"You still smell?"** he asked George.

"Yeah," George admitted. "I wanted to help out Mr. Furstman at the pet store. But when I walked over, even he said I stink too much."

"Wow," Alex said. **"That place smells really nasty. You must reek."**

"It's hard to get rid of this stuff," George told his friend. "I've taken three tomato-juice baths already . . . so I guess Louie can't wait to show the whole school the tape of me getting sprayed, huh?" he asked quietly.

"Oh, you don't have to worry about that," Alex said.

"Isn't he the fourth-grade sportscaster?" George asked.

"No," Alex said. "He hasn't been at school, either. Turns out **there was poison ivy in the woods** where they were hiding. Louie's out until he stops itching. So are Mike and Max."

George smiled. "Awesome!"

"That's cold, dude," Alex said.

"No, I didn't mean it's awesome they have poison ivy," George said. "I meant it's awesome that I still have a chance to be the fourth-grade sportscaster."

"Sorry, dude," Alex said. "They gave the job to someone else."

"Who?" George wondered.

"Julianna," Alex said. "I was at the studio today, learning how to work the cameras, and I saw her audition tape. It was pretty good. She interviewed the teachers about other Field Days, which was a **really smooth move**. Then she talked about how she couldn't wait for baseball season because she could tell from the races that there are some excellent runners in the fourth grade. **She knows a lot about sports.**"

That was the truth. Julianna was easily the best athlete in the fourth grade.

"Julianna will be a good sportscaster," George said. "And maybe I can get her to do a report on skateboarding. I'm practicing some **way-cool, new stunts**."

"You should probably wait," Alex said. "You don't want her to be able to smell your 180 coming before she sees it."

"True," George agreed with a laugh.

A few minutes later, George and Alex hung up. That was when he heard something awful. *Really* **awful.**

His stomach began to grumble. And rumble.

George gulped. Oh no! Was the super burp back again?

He sat there at his desk, waiting for the bing-bonging and ping-ponging to start. But it didn't. There was nothing in George's stomach. In fact, **that was the problem**. George's stomach was rumbling because he was hungry.

"Hey, Mom," he called downstairs, "what's for dinner?"

"Spaghetti and meatballs," his mom answered. **"With tomato sauce."**

Oh man. Now George was going to be tomatoed inside *and* out. Still, he was glad that all he had in his belly right now were hunger pains.

Of course that didn't mean the super burp wouldn't be back. **It could happen any time.** And without any warning. In fact, there was only one thing George could count on when it came to the super burp: When it came, it would cause trouble. And that was *ba-a-ad*!

About the Author

Nancy Krulik is the author of more than 150 books for children and young adults including three *New York Times* best sellers and the popular Katie Kazoo, Switcheroo books. She lives in New York City with her family, and many of George Brown's escapades are based on things her own kids have done. (No one delivers a good burp quite like Nancy's son, Ian!) Nancy's favorite thing to do is laugh, which comes in pretty handy when you're trying to write funny books!

About the Illustrator

Aaron Blecha was raised by a school of giant squid in Wisconsin and now lives with his wife in London, England. He works as an artist and animator designing toys, making cartoons, and illustrating books, including the Zombiekins series. You can enjoy more of his weird creations at www.monstersquid.com.